Charm Hall

AND COMING SOON

Charm Hall

Mona Lisa Mystery

Tabitha Black

Hodder
Children's
Books

A division of Hachette Children's Books

Special thanks to Sue Mongredien

For Abby and Becky French, with lots of love

Copyright © 2007 Working Partners Ltd
Created by Working Partners Limited, London, WC1X 9HH
Illustrations copyright © 2007 Margaret Chamberlain

First published in Great Britain in 2007 by Hodder Children's Books

The rights of Tabitha Black and Margaret Chamberlain to
be identified as the Author and Illustrator of the Work respectively
have been asserted by them in accordance with the
Copyright, Designs and Patents Act 1988

1

A Catalogue record for this book is available from the British Library

ISBN 978 0 340 93143 1

Typeset in Weiss by Avon DataSet Ltd,
Bidford on Avon, Warwickshire

Printed in Great Britain by
Clays Ltd, St Ives plc

The paper and board used in this paperback by Hodder Children's
Books are natural recyclable products made from wood grown in
sustainable forests. The manufacturing processes conform to the
environmental regulations of the country of origin.

Hodder Children's Books
a division of Hachette Children's Books
338 Euston Road, London NW1 3BH
An Hachette Livre UK company

Chapter One

Paige Hart opened her eyes. She was suddenly wide awake. A familiar sound had woken her up, but she couldn't quite remember what it was. It was dark in the attic dormitory, with just a slice of silver moonlight shining through a crack in the curtains. Paige lay there listening to the soft, slow breathing of her dorm-mates, Shannon and Summer, then wriggled into a more comfortable position. Maybe she'd dreamed that she'd heard something.

But then, suddenly, the sound came again. *Miaow!* It was Velvet, the little black kitten who was the girls' secret pet.

Paige sat up and stared around in the darkness. There, on Paige's bedside table, sat Velvet, her golden eyes glowing in the dark. Paige glanced at her alarm clock. It was five minutes to midnight.

"What's up, puss?" she asked Velvet, reaching out to stroke her, but Velvet immediately jumped down from the bedside table and ran swiftly across the room.

Paige watched as Velvet trotted over to Shannon's bed, miaowed loudly, and then used a paw to tap one of Shannon's hands that was dangling over the side of the bed.

Shannon stirred. "Velvet?" she murmured groggily, sitting up. "What's wrong?"

But Velvet was already padding across the carpet to Summer's bed, where she leaped lightly on to the pillow and rubbed her head against Summer's cheek.

Paige was feeling more awake by the second. Velvet was acting very strangely. "Velvet, what is it?" she asked, swinging her legs out of bed and pulling on her dressing gown with a shiver. It was cold and she could hear the wind gusting around the rooftops outside. She flicked on her lamp to see that Velvet was now scrabbling at the door.

"She wants to show us something," Shannon said, now wide awake too. "She's never woken us up like this before, has she?"

"And it's not like she needs *our* help to get in and out of the room," Summer agreed, pushing her bare feet into slippers.

Velvet had come in through the window one day, not long after Paige had started at Charm Hall Boarding School, and Paige and her friends had quickly realized that Velvet was no ordinary black kitten – she had special magical powers!

"So, what are we waiting for?" Shannon asked, grabbing the torch from the drawer of her bedside table. "Let's go!"

Paige felt prickly with excitement. "We'll have to be really quiet," she whispered. "If we get caught, we'll be in big trouble!"

Velvet mewed, as if in agreement, and Summer opened the bedroom door.

Shannon turned on her torch and Velvet led the way, her paws silent on the wooden staircases and along the hallways. To Paige's mind, Velvet looked like an inky shadow, slipping along the corridor. The girls tiptoed after her, through the school, until they reached the back door.

Velvet stood on her hind legs and scratched at the door. The girls exchanged glances.

"You want us to go *outside?*" Summer asked. "In the middle of the night?"

Velvet miaowed loudly.

"I think that was a 'yes'," Paige said. "Come on." She turned the door handle and pushed – but the door stayed firmly shut. "Oh, it's locked!" she whispered disappointedly.

"And it's bolted at the top," Shannon added, shining her torch up to show the others. "How are we going to get out?"

Velvet sat down, whisking her tail from side to side behind her. Her whiskers began to shimmer with a bright golden gleam, and Paige felt a thrill of excitement. She'd seen Velvet's magic many times now, but she still couldn't help being completely mesmerized by it.

A stream of golden sparkles swirled up around Velvet's body, and then zoomed over to the door, fizzing and sparkling like tiny fireflies. The next moment, the bolt slid back silently, and the girls heard the lock clicking open.

Paige tried the door handle again and this time the door swung open easily. "Nice one, Velvet!" she said with a grin, stepping through the dorway. Outside, the frosty ground sparkled silver in the moonlight. "Wow, it's like being in a Christmas card," Paige breathed.

A cold wind snaked around Paige's ankles, and she shivered.

"Brrr," Shannon said, rubbing her arms. "We must be mad, being out in the middle of the night in November!"

Before anyone could reply, Paige heard the faint sound of sobbing, carried on the wind. "Who's that?" she hissed.

Shannon and Summer listened hard. "Well, whoever it is, they're crying their heart out," Summer replied. "Is that why you brought us out here, Velvet? Is someone in trouble?"

Velvet was already picking her way across the terrace, towards the sound of the crying, her tail swaying in the air. The frost crunched under the girls' feet as they followed the little kitten.

Velvet led them to a large, old oak tree and Paige's eyes widened when she saw a little girl crouched at the foot of the tree in the darkness. The girl was sobbing with her head on her knees, but Paige was certain she wasn't a Charm Hall student – she was too young. Paige thought she could only be about five or six years old. So who was she, and where had she come from?

Paige, Summer and Shannon ran over to her.

"Hello," Paige said, kneeling down beside the little girl. "What's wrong?"

The little girl didn't reply.

Summer and Shannon crouched down next to Paige. "What are you doing out here?" Summer asked the little girl gently.

The little girl looked up, her dark eyes swollen from crying. "I was trying to run away," she said mournfully.

Velvet walked over and pushed her little black head against the girl's hand. The girl gave a surprised smile as she saw Velvet. "Hello, kitty," she said, stroking Velvet, who immediately let out a rumbling purr.

Shannon put her arm around the little girl. "I'm

Shannon," she said. "And this is Velvet. What's your name? And why were you trying to run away?"

"I'm Lily," the little girl replied, wiping her tears away with the back of one hand. Velvet clambered into her lap, still purring, and Lily stroked her. "I'm staying with my Grandpa Sam," she went on. "He works at the school. But I don't want to live here. I want to go home to my mum and dad!"

Something clicked in Paige's head. "Sam – do you mean the caretaker?" she asked. "He has a cottage around here, doesn't he?"

Lily nodded. "Yes," she said, staring down at Velvet. "Mum and Dad say I have to stay with him while they . . . 'sort things out'." She bit her lip. "They've been arguing a lot, and Dad went away for a few days. Then he came back, and . . ." she sighed, "they said I had to come here. But I want to go home. I miss them – and my friends too."

"That sounds rough," Summer said sympathetically. "But you shouldn't be out here in the cold."

"Your grandpa will be dead worried if he finds you've gone," Shannon added. "We'd better take you back to his house. Hopefully your mum and dad will soon sort things out." Shannon got to her feet and held out a hand to Lily.

Velvet jumped off Lily's lap, and the young girl got to her feet. "I didn't mean to make Grandpa Sam upset," she said. "I just . . ."

"Don't worry," Paige assured her. "He'll just be glad to have you back safe and sound. Now, let's go. It's freezing!"

Chapter Two

The four girls and Velvet headed along the path and across the lawn to the caretaker's cottage. As they approached, the door burst open and Sam strode out.

"Lily!" he called frantically, pulling on a coat. Paige could see his breath steaming in the cold air. "Lily!"

"It's all right, she's here!" Shannon called, as the girls and Velvet stepped out of the darkness and into the pool of light near the cottage. "We found her!"

Sam ran towards the girls, looking very relieved.

He picked up Lily and held her close to him. "Lily! Thank goodness you're all right! Where have you been?"

"I wanted to go home," Lily replied in a muffled voice. "I'm s-s-sorry, Grandpa."

"Oh, Lily!" Sam said, sounding very sad. "I know it's hard, being away from home, but I'm sure it won't be for long. How about you give your mum a ring in the morning and have a good chat?"

Lily nodded and Sam kissed the top of her head and put her down on the ground. Then he straightened up and looked over at Paige, Shannon and Summer. He recognized them straight away, as he'd taken them on a trip, not long ago, to meet Mrs Brightman, a former teacher and pupil at Charm Hall School.

"Thank you, girls," he said. "I don't know what I'd have done if—" He broke off, his eyes misty. "What were you three doing outside in the middle of the night anyway?" he asked. "You're meant to be in bed!"

"We . . . We heard someone crying," Paige explained quickly. After all, that much was true.

"And we followed the sound, and found Lily," Shannon put in.

Sam looked down at his granddaughter. "Come on, pickle, let's get you in the warm," he said. Then he turned back to Paige, Shannon and Summer. "Why don't you all come in and warm up? I'll make some hot chocolate, and then I'll walk you back to the school." Sam pointed at Velvet. "You can even bring your furry friend!"

Paige nodded gratefully, and scooped Velvet up into her arms. She wouldn't have liked to leave the kitten outside on a night like this. "Thanks, that would be lovely," she said.

She and her friends followed Sam into the cottage. Paige felt Velvet purr contentedly in her arms. "You *are* clever," she whispered in the kitten's ear. "Well done, Velvet!"

Sam made everyone steaming mugs of hot chocolate, and even poured a saucer of milk for Velvet. After she'd lapped it up, Velvet curled up in front of Sam's wood fire, gazing into the flames.

"Sweet, isn't she?" Sam commented. "I wonder who owns her."

Paige and her friends exchanged glances. They

weren't supposed to keep pets at Charm Hall, so they really didn't want to admit that Velvet lived in their dorm!

"Oh, she must live somewhere nearby," Shannon said vaguely.

Paige quickly changed the subject. "I think Lily's dozed off," she said. The little girl had curled up on the sofa next to Sam, and nodded off in the warmth from the fire.

Sam scooped her up without waking her. "Let's pop you in bed," he murmured, carrying her out of the room.

"Poor lass," he said when he returned. "She's really missing her parents, and I . . ." He shrugged awkwardly. "Well, it's been a long time since I've had to look after a child. We're both struggling a bit, to be honest."

"I'm sure she'll settle in soon," Summer said encouragingly.

Sam nodded, but he didn't look convinced. "She's been taken out of her usual school for the time being, and is going to the local one, in the village," he told the girls. "Hopefully, she'll feel a bit happier when she's made some friends there."

Paige rubbed her eyes, suddenly feeling very sleepy, and Sam put his mug down. "Sorry," he said. "Here I am, keeping you from your beds. Come on, I'll walk you back to school before you fall asleep in front of the fire."

"I've got an exciting announcement to make," Miss Montgomery, the girls' music teacher, said the next morning.

Paige had been feeling pretty tired after last night's adventure, but her music teacher's words woke her up.

"There's going to be an Inter-school Christmas carol competition next month," Miss Montgomery went on, "to be held at the Churchill School. Six schools are going to be competing – including Charm Hall."

Paige noticed Shannon's eyes light up at this news. She knew her friend loved singing.

"Now, we have lots of fine singers in our school, and only twelve places in the choir," Miss Montgomery went on. "So, to make it fair, we're holding try-outs in a week's time. One girl from each year will be chosen to sit on the judging panel and that panel will help select our choir. At lunchtime today, Miss Linnet will pick six names out of a hat to form the panel."

Shannon grinned at her friends. "I'm definitely going to audition for the choir!" she whispered excitedly. "It will be just like one of those reality TV shows. They should call it *Carol Idol!*" she joked.

"Or the *Xmas Factor!*" Paige laughed.

Abigail Carter, who was sitting nearby, chipped in. "Shame that you've got the *non-factor* when it comes to singing, Shannon Carroll," she said cattily.

"Not true!" Paige retorted. "Shannon's a brilliant singer!"

"You're just jealous, Abigail," Summer added.

Abigail tossed her hair and opened her mouth to reply, but Miss Montgomery was clapping her hands for silence.

"Quiet, please!" she called. "We're going to spend today's lesson choosing our favourite carols and practising them. This will get everyone in the mood for the try-outs. So . . . any suggestions? What shall we sing first?"

Mia West, a friend of Abigail's, put her hand up. "*Silent Night!*" she said.

Miss Montgomery smiled at her. "A good choice, Mia." She picked up a pile of booklets and passed them around. *"Silent Night* is on page ten," she told the class.

When everyone was ready, Miss Montgomery sat down at the piano in the corner and played the first chord.

"Si-i-i-i-lent night . . ." everyone began to sing.

As the girls sang the first verse, Paige couldn't help but notice how clear Shannon's voice sounded. *Shannon is such a good singer*, Paige thought to herself. *I really hope she gets picked for the choir!*

Chapter Three

Later that day, on their way to the dining hall, the three girls saw Miss Linnet, the headteacher, who promptly beckoned them over. Paige felt jittery as she and her friends went across to join Miss Linnet. Had Sam told the head that they'd been out in the school grounds last night? Nice as Miss Linnet was, Paige knew she wouldn't be at all happy to hear that the girls had been out of their room after lights out.

"Hello, girls," Miss Linnet said cheerfully. "I was speaking to Sam this morning about his little granddaughter, Lily. I believe you've met her?"

"Um . . . yes," Paige replied tentatively, biting her lip at the mention of Sam.

"I think Sam also told you that Lily is going through a difficult period at the moment," Miss Linnet went on. The girls all nodded. "Well, I was wondering if you three would be kind enough to spend a little time with Lily, and try to make her feel more settled while she's here. Apparently, she really enjoyed meeting you all, and was chattering about you non-stop over breakfast."

"Sure, no problem," Shannon said.

"We'll pop in and see her after school," Summer volunteered.

Miss Linnet smiled at them. "That would be very nice of you," she said. "I'm sure Sam *and* Lily will really appreciate it."

She walked away, and Paige let out a sigh of relief. "Phew," she said. "I thought we were about to get told off for being out last night!"

"Me too," Summer said, running her hand nervously through her hair. "But I think we got away with it."

The three friends got their lunch and sat down to eat. It seemed as if everyone was talking about the Christmas carol competition, and the judging panel.

"I hope *I'm* on the panel," Paige heard Abigail say to Mia. "I've got an excellent ear for music, you know."

Shannon rolled her eyes at Paige and Summer. "Of course she has," she muttered. "Because, as everyone knows, Abigail Carter is excellent at *everything*."

"Everything except modesty," Summer put in. "She's not so hot on that!"

At that moment, Miss Linnet came into the dining hall carrying a large wooden box, and stood at the front of the room. "Can I have your attention, please?" she said.

Silence fell at once. Every girl knew what was coming. The judging panel for the choir try-outs was about to be selected!

Miss Linnet held up the box. "I have six bags in here," she said. "Each represents a different year group, and contains all the names of students from that year. I will select, at random, one name from each bag – and those six girls will form the judging panel to choose the best singers for the choir. The

18

choir will then rehearse three carols for next month's competition. Now, it is no easy task judging your peers, so I want lots of support for the girls who are chosen. And of course, if I call out your name and you would actually like to try out for the choir yourself, just let me know and I'll draw out an alternative name."

Paige watched the headteacher pick up the first bag and plunge her hand into it. Paige almost expected a drum roll, the atmosphere was so tense.

"First on the panel, representing Year Five, is . . ." Miss Linnet pulled out a name. "Amelia Sanchez! Where are you, Amelia?"

There was a round of applause as a pretty, dark-haired Year Five girl stood up, blushing.

"Right, next up are the Year Six girls," Miss Linnet said, picking up another bag and plunging her hand into it. "The second person on the panel is . . . Abigail Carter!"

"YES!" cheered Abigail loudly, punching the air. A scattering of applause followed. Paige put her hands together and reluctantly clapped too. *Oh, great*, she thought. *We'll never hear the end of this!*

Miss Linnet went through each year group, picking out names until the panel was complete. "Try-outs for the choir will be at the end of the week," she announced. "And I wish you all the best of luck!"

Most people were chattering excitedly as they left the dining hall to collect their books for afternoon lessons, but Shannon looked glum.

"Well, that's me stuffed then," she sighed. "There's no way I'll ever get in the choir if

Abigail Carter is on the selection committee. No way on earth!"

"Come on," Paige said encouragingly. "Abigail is only one person on the panel. There are five others."

"*And* Miss Montgomery," Summer reminded them. "And she *loves* your voice."

"Yeah, but you know what Abigail's like," Shannon said. "I don't think there's much point in me trying out at all. She'll only manage to make some horrible remark about my voice and turn the others against me, you wait and see."

"She can try, Shannon, but that doesn't mean she'll succeed," Summer said staunchly.

"I agree. You can't let Abigail stop you trying out for the choir, Shannon," Paige put in. "You're too good to give up before the try-outs have even started."

Shannon thought for a moment, and then nodded, a determined glint in her eye. "You're right," she said. "I'm not going to let Abigail Carter stand in my way!"

After school that day Paige, Shannon and Summer

headed straight over to Sam's cottage to visit Lily. Sam showed them into the living room, where Lily was sitting, rather forlornly, in front of a small Christmas tree.

"Ooh, nice," Shannon said, going over and stroking a dark-green branch. "This is the first Christmas tree I've seen all year." She sniffed one of the branches with a grin. "It smells of Christmas!"

"Are you going to decorate it?" Paige asked Lily.

Lily shrugged miserably and Sam looked awkward. "I know it's a bit early for a Christmas tree, but I thought it might cheer Lily up," he explained. Suddenly he looked rather forlorn himself. He looked over at the girls and mouthed, "Only it seems to have made things worse."

Paige glanced at the downcast expression on Lily's face, and wondered if the tree was making her think about Christmases back home. Paige knew that she would have missed her own parents and friends if she'd had to stay with her grandpa when she'd been Lily's age. It must be even harder with Christmas around the corner.

"Have you got any decorations or lights Lily could put on the tree?" she asked Sam.

"Christmas trees look so much prettier when they're all twinkly and sparkly," Summer added, with an encouraging smile at Lily.

"Well, I bought some paper strips for making paper chains," Sam said, indicating the packs on the table. "But I don't have any tree decorations here in the cottage," he went on. Then his face brightened. "Although I *do* know where there are some spare baubles and lights up at the school. I don't suppose you three could stay here with Lily for five minutes, while I nip up and get them, could you?"

"No probs," Shannon said, settling down on the rug.

"We'll get started on the paper chains with Lily," Paige added. She looped one of the paper strips around her finger to make a circle and then dangled it from one of her ears, like a colourful earring. "What do you think? Does this colour suit me?"

Lily started to giggle.

"That's a sound I haven't heard for a while!" Sam said, sounding relieved. "I'll be back in a flash."

"Right," Shannon said, grabbing a few bundles of the paper strips and handing them out. "Let's see who can make the longest chain. Ready, steady, go!"

"Hang on, I wasn't ready," Summer laughed, rushing to open the packet in her hand. "Come on, Lily! We can't let Shannon beat us. Her head's big enough already!"

"Oi, watch it!" Shannon retorted. She licked the sticky end of one of her strips and stuck it to Summer's forehead. "Any more lip from you and I might have to gag you with a paper chain."

Paige smiled as Lily laughed out loud at the indignant look on Summer's face. "And I'll chain *you* to the Christmas tree, Shannon Carroll, if you don't watch out!" Summer said, brandishing a paper strip threateningly.

It wasn't long before all the girls had made long paper chains. "Here, Lily, a lovely rainbow scarf for you," Shannon said, winding her paper chain around Lily's shoulders. "Oh, *dahling*, you look fabulous!" she told the little girl, who was giggling.

Summer smiled. "Paper chains are all the rage this Christmas!" she told Lily.

"You know, we should definitely make some of these for our dorm," Paige said.

"Ooh, yes," Summer agreed, "and we've got our stockings to start thinking about as well, remember?"

"Stockings?" Paige asked curiously. She hadn't been at Charm Hall as long as her friends, and this was her first Christmas term at the school.

"Oh, it's this really fun school tradition," Summer explained. "Everyone hangs up a stocking in the last week of term, and your dorm-mates make or buy little presents to put in it for you."

Just then, Sam walked in with a box of tree decorations. "Here we are," he said, setting the box down. "I'll make us some tea. Give me a shout if you need a hand."

Lily's eyes lit up as she saw the strings of colourful tinsel and bright glass baubles heaped in the box. "Ooh, fairy lights," she said, pulling out a string. "Look!"

Paige and her friends exchanged pleased glances. Lily was *definitely* looking more cheerful now!

The four of them draped tinsel and lights around the tree, and hung the baubles from its branches.

"Right, that's the lot," Summer said, pulling the last piece of silver tinsel from the box. "Oh, no, wait, here's an angel for the top. Isn't she gorgeous?"

They all stopped what they were doing to inspect the angel. She had gauzy wings, a silvery dress and a halo.

Shannon, who was the tallest, tied her carefully to the top of the tree. "There!" she exclaimed, standing back. "What do you think of that then, Lily?"

But Paige saw that Lily was looking sad again. "What is it?" she asked the little girl. "Don't you like the angel?"

Lily shook her head. "It's not that," she said. "It's just . . ." her shoulders slumped, "I was supposed to be the angel in my school nativity play, only I can't be any more, not now that I've changed school."

"What part have you got at your new school?" Paige asked.

"I'm just in the choir," Lily said quietly. "All the parts had already been given out."

Shannon smiled encouragingly. "Hey! Nothing wrong with being in the choir," she said. "I'm hoping to be in my school's choir."

Just then Sam called from the kitchen. "Lily! Could you help me choose some cakes?"

Lily ran through to the kitchen, and Paige and her friends looked at one another.

"It's a shame Lily can't be an angel in the play," Paige said, her eyes flicking up to the angel on the tree.

"Well, at least she has a nice tree now. Let's turn the lights on, so that Lily has a nice surprise when she comes back in," Shannon suggested, crouching down to turn on the lights at the socket. "Ready, everyone? Three . . . two . . . one!" Shannon flicked the switch . . . but nothing happened.

"Is one of the bulbs loose?" Paige asked. Shannon flicked the power off again, then she and Paige went round, making sure that all the bulbs were firmly screwed in.

Shannon turned the power back on. Still nothing.

"Oh, no! The lights must be broken!" Summer groaned.

"Lily's going to be gutted," Shannon added.

Paige was silent, wondering if there was anything they could do to fix the lights. But then Summer suddenly pointed at the window. "Look who's here!" she cried.

Paige turned to see Velvet's little face peeping in through the glass. "Oh, Velvet," Paige said, going over to open the window and let her in. "Perfect timing!"

Chapter Four

Velvet jumped in through the window and immediately trotted over to the tree. As the girls watched, the kitten surveyed the tree with wide amber eyes. Then her tail began to swish back and forth.

Paige held her breath as Velvet's whiskers shimmered with their familiar golden gleam, and a moment later a blizzard of tiny multicoloured sparkles went whizzing and whirling around the Christmas tree! Paige stared in amazement as the sparkles swirled around every bauble and piece of tinsel, making them glow and twinkle until the whole tree seemed to be shimmering and sparkling. Then, with a last rainbow swirl, the bright sparkles danced along the string of fairy lights, which suddenly burst into light, glittering and twinkling like little colourful stars.

Paige blinked as the magic sparkles vanished. "Oh, wow!" she cried. "It's gorgeous!"

It was truly the most fantastic, glittery Christmas tree Paige had ever seen! The baubles reflected the

fairy lights, and the whole tree seemed to be shining with colour and light.

"Velvet!" Shannon breathed. "That looks . . ."

". . . brilliant!" Summer finished for her with a grin. She leaned down to stroke the little cat, whose whiskers had returned to their usual colour once more.

"Oh!" came a gasp from behind them. The girls turned to see Lily coming through from the kitchen, her eyes wide with delight. "Grandpa, come and see!" she called, jumping up and down with excitement. "Come and see!"

Sam followed, carrying a tray of tea and cakes. "Hey! Isn't that lovely?" he said admiringly. "I've never *seen* such sparkly fairy lights! Well done, all of you. It looks *very* festive in here now."

Sam poured everyone some tea, and handed around cakes. Then he caught sight of Velvet stalking some threads of golden tinsel that had fallen on the carpet. "That cat again!" he smiled. "Where did she come from?"

"She came in through the window," Paige answered truthfully.

Sam stroked Velvet, and Lily wriggled off the

sofa to pet her too. She plucked a bauble off the tree and dangled it above Velvet's head, and the kitten stood on her back legs to bat it. "She is *so* cute," Lily said happily. "Look, Grandpa! She's trying to hit it!"

Sam smiled, and turned to the girls. "Are you three *sure* she's not yours? She always seems to appear when you do," he said.

Shannon laughed. "Yes, well, you know this is *really* yummy cake," she said, quickly changing the subject.

Lily went back to the sofa, and Velvet followed, jumping on to Lily's lap and nudging Lily's hand with her head. Lily looked thrilled, and carefully began stroking the kitten.

Sam leaned over to pet Velvet too. "Did your mum ever tell you about the kitten she used to have when she was about your age?" he asked Lily.

"No," Lily replied, looking up in interest.

"Georgie, we called her," Sam said. "She was such a scamp! Always climbing the curtains, and perching on the curtain rail. And whenever your mum walked past she'd give this great leap and try to land on her shoulder." He grinned.

"Your mum's screams as Georgie landed on her were quite something!"

Lily giggled. "What else did Georgie do?"

Sam leaned back on the sofa. "What else? Oh, lots of things. Let me see now . . ."

Paige and her friends exchanged smiles as Sam told Lily tales of Georgie the kitten. Paige couldn't resist leaning forward to stroke Velvet, who was comfortably curled up on Lily's lap. Clever Velvet hadn't just worked her magic with the fairy lights – she seemed to be bringing Lily and her grandpa closer together too.

The day of the Christmas carol try-outs came around quickly, and that lunchtime Paige and Summer walked to the music room with Shannon. They had decided to go along and cheer their friend on, especially since Shannon had an awful cold and was feeling a bit nervous.

"Why don't you two give it go?" Shannon asked, then promptly sneezed into her tissue.

Neither Paige nor Summer were taking part. Paige could keep in tune, but knew that her voice was a little thin and reedy, and Summer had cheerfully declared that she couldn't carry a tune to save her life.

Summer snorted. "Gymnastics and swimming – yes. Singing in a carol concert – no," she said in a matter-of-fact way.

Paige grinned. "I'm with you there," she agreed. "Competing in the try-outs – no way. Going to watch Shannon blast away the opposition – yes, definitely!"

"I'm glad *you're* so confident," Shannon said, blowing her nose as they neared the music room. "I can't believe I've gone and caught a cold right before the try-outs. I hope I don't sound too bunged up when I'm singing."

The girls went into the room and Paige saw that a long table had been set up, with Miss Montgomery and the six members of the judging panel sitting along it. There were about twenty other girls from Years Five and Six waiting to audition too. The try-outs were being spread out through the day, with the older girls getting a chance to sing after school. Paige noticed that Shannon turned rather pale at the sight of all the other girls, but she still managed to walk coolly across the room to take a seat.

Paige felt a twist of annoyance as Abigail smirked at them from her place on the panel.

"We're not auditioning for *groups* today," Abigail said nastily.

"We're not—" Paige began crossly, but Shannon calmly interrupted.

"Paige and Summer have just come to give me some moral support, Abs. No biggie," she announced.

Abigail glared at Shannon. "It's Abigail to you, not 'Abs'," she said haughtily.

"Whatever," Shannon sighed, and Paige had to stifle a giggle. Only Shannon would dare call Abigail Carter "Abs"!

Miss Montgomery clapped her hands for quiet. "Before we begin, I just want to let you know that the girls who are picked for the choir will be required to rehearse every Wednesday and Friday after school, up until the date of the competition, which is December 13th. The names of the girls who have been chosen will be announced at dinner time. But we've got a lot of singing to listen to before we can make any decisions, so who's first?"

Paige and her friends watched as, one by one,

the waiting girls stood up in front of the panel and sang a carol.

Abigail seemed to be taking her position on the panel very seriously. She frowned at the quality of some of the singing, winced at any missed notes, and made rude comments in whispers to the rest of the panel. "Oh *dear*, we're looking for a voice that soars not trembles," she said about one Year Five girl who was so nervous her voice wobbled all over the place.

"I don't *think* so!" she spluttered, as another girl missed every note in *The Holly and the Ivy*.

Paige and Summer were sitting near Abigail's end of the panel, so they could hear every word of her criticisms. Paige glanced at Miss Montgomery, hoping the teacher would tell Abigail to be quiet, but the teacher was out of earshot.

Before long it was Shannon's turn, and Paige crossed her fingers. Shannon and Abigail weren't exactly best friends but Paige really hoped Abigail wouldn't make any nasty comments about Shannon's singing.

"Here we go," Summer whispered, clutching Paige's hand as their friend cleared her throat.

"O little town of Bethlehem,

How still we see thee lie . . ." sang Shannon.

Even with a cold Shannon was good, Paige thought happily. Her voice was a bit huskier than usual, but it still rang out strongly and she didn't miss a note.

As the last notes died away, Paige and Summer both burst into applause. "Go, Shannon!" Paige cheered.

Shannon turned and grinned at them, then faced the panel once more. "I've got a bit of a cold, I'm afraid, so—" she began.

"We're not interested in excuses," Abigail interrupted. She turned to the Year Eight girl, Vivien, who was next to her on the panel. "Not much *stage presence*, if you ask me."

"Abigail, that's enough," Miss Montgomery snapped, giving her a warning look. "Thank you, Shannon."

"It was a pleasure, Miss Montgomery," Shannon said sweetly. Then she turned to Abigail. "What was that about stage presence, Abs?" she asked, raising an eyebrow. "Do you want me to dance as well as sing, maybe? Make the stage my own?"

"Well, no, I didn't say—" Abigail protested, but Shannon had already started belting out a catchy pop tune, and performing an impressive twirl on the spot.

"That'll do, Shannon," Miss Montgomery said with a smile, as the room erupted in laughter and applause. "Who's next?"

Shannon grinned at Abigail, who had turned very pink, and marched out of the room. Paige and Summer rushed after her.

They found Shannon leaning against the wall of

the corridor, looking very annoyed. "I shouldn't have let her get to me," Shannon said, frowning. "But she just wound me up so much with her stupid comments! And now I probably won't get picked for the competition, because the panel will think I'm a bit loopy."

"Are you kidding?" Paige retorted. "They loved your singing, and Miss Montgomery was definitely smiling at the end of it!"

Shannon's mouth twitched suddenly and she laughed. "Abigail's face was a picture, wasn't it? It was almost worth not getting into the choir just to see that!"

"I thought her eyes were going to pop out!" Summer giggled. "And I'm sure you won't get left out of the choir."

"Summer's right," Paige agreed. "They'd be mad not to pick you!"

Shannon shrugged. "I just can't see Miss Montgomery letting me in now," she sighed. "Oh, well, me and my big mouth!"

Chapter Five

The girls had an art lesson with Miss Arnold next, and they were careful to choose a desk well away from Abigail.

Miss Arnold split the class into groups of three or four, and handed out a copy of a famous painting to each group. Paige, Shannon and Summer were in a group together, and were given a picture of the *Mona Lisa*.

"I'd like you all to turn over your pictures and read the question on the back, please," Miss Arnold said.

There was much rustling as everyone flipped their pictures over.

"Why is the *Mona Lisa* smiling?" Summer read aloud to Paige and Shannon.

"Miss Collins and I have put together a project for you this term," Miss Arnold said. "In your English lessons, Miss Collins will be asking you to write a short story to answer the question on the back of your picture. She'll go through that with you in more detail in your next lesson." She smiled around the room. "In your art lessons, you'll be doing modern interpretations of the piece of art I have given you. You can use any materials you like – paint, pastels, chalks – it's up to you. Today, I'd like you to start making preliminary sketches. What does the picture say to you? How are you going to reproduce it with a modern twist?"

As Miss Arnold finished speaking, the classroom buzzed with conversation. Paige leaned over the *Mona Lisa* for a closer look. "Hmmm," she said. "The colours are a bit drab, aren't they? Perhaps the *Mona Lisa* could be livened up with a fluorescent background . . ."

"Or some funky, twenty-first-century clothes," Summer suggested. "And as for her hair – we've got

41

to sort that out for her. A few highlights, maybe? Or even a completely new style?"

Paige grinned as she opened up her sketch book. Then she glanced over at Shannon. Her friend was being very quiet. Normally Shannon would have loads of ideas for something like this, but right now she appeared to be in a world of her own.

"Hey! Earth to Shannon," Paige said, giving her friend a nudge. "Are you still thinking about the choir?"

Shannon nodded. "I'm trying not to," she sighed. "But I don't think I'll be able to think about anything else until I've heard who's got in!"

Silence settled over the dining hall that evening as Miss Montgomery got to her feet. "First, I want to say a big thank-you to everyone who tried out for our choir," she began. "It was a very difficult decision process, but I'm delighted to announce that we have chosen the twelve people who will form the choir." She pushed her glasses up her nose and looked down at a piece of paper she was holding. "In no particular order, the girls are . . ."

Paige let out a squeak as Shannon clutched her hand a bit too tightly. "Sorry," Shannon murmured, not taking her eyes off the music teacher.

"Holly Davies, Anna Brown, Sophie Graham, Hannah Linford, Emily Bates, Sasha Williams . . ."

Shannon had her eyes shut now, as if she couldn't bear to look.

"Serena Velasquez, Isabelle Farnham, Laura Morris, Neela Choudhury, Amy Constantine and . . ." Miss Montgomery squinted at her handwriting, ". . . Shannon Carroll."

"Yes!" squealed Shannon, opening her eyes and looking ecstatic.

"You did it!" cheered Paige.

"Yay!" cried Summer.

There was a round of applause, and cheers of delight from all the girls who'd been picked for the choir. Paige saw Abigail shoot Shannon a particularly sour look, as if *she* didn't think Shannon should have been chosen. But luckily Shannon was too happy to notice.

"This definitely calls for some celebratory chocolate in the dorm tonight," Shannon said. "And I can't wait to tell my mum and dad!"

* * *

"Hey! It's snowing!" Paige heard Belinda Osbourne say excitedly in their English lesson the next day.

There was a scrape of chairs as everyone in the class turned to the window to see the snowflakes tumbling down from the sky.

"All right, girls, it'll probably still be there at break time," their teacher, Miss Collins, laughed. "I want you to get into your groups now, and start thinking up ideas for your short story in the combined English/art project. Just to recap, you need to answer the question on the back of your picture in a story form. Try to get as many ideas as you can from the artwork. Look at all the tiny details, make up stories about the figures in the background, if there are any. See if you can work out the season, and time of day, from any clues there are in the picture. And have fun with it!"

Paige and her friends stared down at the *Mona Lisa*, trying to get some inspiration for story ideas, but the snow had soon stolen their attention.

"I love the way a snowflake tastes when you catch it on your tongue," Shannon said dreamily.

"I hope it settles," Summer added, leaning over her desk to get a better look out of the window. "Then we could have a snowball fight."

"Or build a snowman," Paige said excitedly.

Shannon nodded. "Joan would definitely give us a carrot from the kitchens to use as the nose."

"Come on, guys," Summer said, gazing at the *Mona Lisa* again. "Why do you think she was smiling?"

"Because she'd been picked for the carol concert choir?" Shannon suggested at once.

Paige elbowed her friend good-naturedly. "What *else* might she have been happy about?"

"Maybe she'd just heard a really, really funny joke," Summer replied, her forehead creasing as she thought. "A really hilarious joke that went like this . . ." She frowned. "Hmm, can either of you think of a funny joke?"

"Nope," Shannon said, her face screwed up in concentration. "That always happens when you need to tell a joke!"

Summer nodded. "To be honest, I'm not sure her smile is broad enough for a joke."

"You're right, Summer," Paige agreed. "I think she's smiling about something more romantic."

Shannon picked up her pencil. "Come on, girls, let's get our thinking caps on!"

The girls still hadn't hit upon a convincing reason for the Mona Lisa's smile by the time the bell went for the end of the lesson. Paige looked outside and saw that the snow was still falling thick and fast. "We've got to go out in the snow," Paige declared. "Just for a few minutes."

"Brrr, you must be mad," Mia shivered, overhearing Paige. "I'm going up to my nice cosy dorm to play on my PSP before homework period starts."

"You don't know what you're missing, Mia," Summer laughed, as the girls left the classroom.

Paige and her friends headed straight outside and over to the school's herb garden. The snow was falling faster now, and Paige felt almost dizzy standing there, watching the flakes swirl around her face and land on her coat.

"It's a shame the Mona Lisa wasn't sitting there in a big warm coat and bobble hat, with snow falling behind her," Shannon joked. "Because then we'd *definitely* know why she was smiling. I love snow!"

There was a rustle from a nearby bush, and snow

cascaded from its leaves as Velvet appeared from behind it and padded towards the girls. She jumped on to the sundial that stood in the middle of the garden, her dainty paws leaving little tracks in the snow that had settled there.

"Hello, Velvet!" Paige said, going to stroke her. "Have you got any good ideas about why the Mona Lisa was smiling?"

"We're a bit stuck," Summer explained, tickling the little cat under the chin.

"Hey!" said Shannon suddenly. "Look at Velvet's whiskers!"

Paige's heartbeat quickened as she saw that Velvet's whiskers were glowing brightly with a golden gleam. Then, as Velvet's tail flicked back and forth, Paige suddenly felt as if the herb garden was spinning around her, making everything blurry.

"What's happening?" she heard Summer ask anxiously. "Why is the garden spinning?"

"I don't know!" Shannon replied, grabbing Paige's hand. "But we're about to find out!"

Paige fumbled for Summer's hand on her other side. "Hold tight!" she yelled.

Chapter Six

Paige felt as if she was spinning through the air very fast. A moment later, the spinning sensation slowed and then stopped, and she gradually got her balance. She gazed around curiously.

She and her friends were standing in a busy cobbled street, with a horse and cart just a few metres away from them. The buildings were tall and narrow, some with ornate balconies, and people were bustling to and fro along the road in old-fashioned clothes.

Shocked, Paige stared down at her own clothes to see that they had changed too. Instead of her

school uniform and coat, she now wore a long, slate-grey dress that fell almost to her ankles, and heavy shoes on her feet. Shannon wore a dull green dress, and Summer was in . . .

"Brown! Ugh! How come I get the brown dress?" Summer exclaimed. "I look like I'm wearing a sack!"

Paige giggled at Summer's indignant face. "Where are we?" she said, staring at the unfamiliar surroundings. She could smell baking bread, and wood smoke – and horses, too, now she came to think of it.

"No idea." Shannon whistled. "This is *weird*!"

"It doesn't feel like the twenty-first century," Summer said thoughtfully. "It doesn't even *sound* like the twenty-first century. Listen! No cars, no mobile phones, no aeroplanes . . ."

"It's like England might have been hundreds of years ago," Paige said. Then a thought struck her and she gasped. "Do you think we've travelled back in time?"

An answering mew from somewhere near her feet made Paige think that her guess was right. Velvet was winding herself around Paige's legs, looking very pleased with herself.

"Where are we, Velvet?" Shannon asked, bending down to stroke the kitten. "Hey!" She jumped as a book went whistling past her head, and Velvet skittered away around a corner. "Where did that come from?"

The three friends looked up to see a young dark-haired woman standing on a balcony. She was throwing all sorts of things – books, sheets of paper, even a bunch of faded flowers – out on to the street.

"Do we know her?" Summer asked, staring at the woman. "She looks familiar somehow."

Before Paige or Shannon could reply, a cry went up from a young man with a small lute-like instrument strung over his shoulder, who was dodging the flying objects. "Please, Luisa. I beg you! I'm sorry!"

"I'm not interested!" the woman retorted. "For you to tell me you have spent all your money on a musical instrument, rather than on a birthday present for me – pah! It is over, Antonio. Take your things and go!" She threw a last book at Antonio's head, and then went back inside the house, slamming the balcony doors behind her.

Almost as soon as the doors had shut, they were flung open again and a man wearing a paint-splattered smock appeared. He had intense dark eyes and a pointed nose. "You heard her! Now, don't come back!" he told Antonio. "I am trying to paint a masterpiece, and your shouts for forgiveness are *very* distracting!" He flounced back inside, and again the balcony doors slammed shut.

Antonio looked crestfallen. Paige felt sorry for

him and bent down to pick up one of the books which had landed by her feet.

"Here," she said, handing him the book. "I'm Paige, by the way."

"Antonio," the man told her sadly. "Thank you."

The girls helped Antonio gather up his belongings. "Um, Antonio," Shannon said as they did so. "I know that this is going to sound a bit strange, but would you mind telling me what the date is? And, er . . . where we are?"

Antonio gave her an odd look before replying. "It is 1504, of course. And we are in Italy!" he told her.

"Italy?" Summer echoed, her blue eyes wide. "But I can't speak Italian!"

"I think you can now," Shannon said drily.

"It must be part of the magic," Paige whispered. "But what are we doing here?"

Shannon shrugged and turned back to Antonio. "Who was that woman up there? Did you say her name was Luisa?"

"Luisa, yes, although I call her my sweet Lisa. She is the love of my life," Antonio sighed. "But she is very angry that I didn't buy her a birthday present. You see, I am a musician, and I got distracted by this mandolin," he explained, taking the small lute-like instrument off his shoulder and looking at it sorrowfully. "I had to have it. After all, how can I be a musician without a musical instrument to play? But then I had no money left for Luisa's present."

"So who was that guy in the smock?" Summer asked as they finished gathering Antonio's things. "Is he Luisa's dad?"

Antonio laughed and shook his head. "No," he said. "Didn't you recognize him? That was Leonardo da Vinci!"

Paige stared at him in shock. "Did you just say Leonardo da Vinci?" she asked.

"Yes," Antonio replied, sounding despondent. "You have heard of him, yes? He is a very successful painter. I am sure my sweet Lisa will fall in love with him!"

A sudden gust of wind sent some sheets of paper flying out of Antonio's hand and up the street. Antonio chased after them, and the girls stared at one another.

"So, Antonio's 'sweet Lisa' must be the *Mona*

Lisa!" Summer exclaimed. "No wonder she looked familiar!"

"I bet that's why Velvet brought us here," Paige added with a grin. "To find out the real reason behind the *Mona Lisa*'s smile!"

Shannon laughed out loud. "I knew Velvet was special, but this is super cool!" she declared.

Paige looked around to see if Velvet was nearby, but the kitten was nowhere to be seen. Paige wasn't worried though. She was sure that Velvet would be just fine, wherever she was. After all, she was a *magical* cat.

Summer gazed up at Luisa's balcony. "Well, Luisa doesn't seem to be doing a lot of smiling at the moment," she said. "Unless Antonio's right, and she's in love with Leonardo da Vinci. Maybe she's up there smiling at *him!*"

"We're never going to get to see Luisa while she's sitting for her portrait, though," Paige said thoughtfully. She glanced over at Antonio. "Maybe we should stick with Antonio for a while. He might know a way for us to meet her properly."

Shannon nodded. "Here he comes, let's ask him."

"I must thank you for your help, ladies," Antonio

said, struggling to pick up all his possessions at once. "It was a delight to meet you."

"Wait! We can help you carry your things, if you like," Paige said quickly, as she, Summer and Shannon stepped forward to take some items from Antonio.

Antonio smiled gratefully at the suggestion. "Well, if it's not too much trouble, that would be most helpful. My home is not far," he told them. "This way . . ."

Antonio lived in the next street. A woman was scrubbing the front step when they approached the house, and she straightened up, smiling at the girls. "Hello!" she said. "Who are your friends, Antonio?"

"Hello, I'm Paige," Paige said stepping forward.

"And I'm Shannon," Shannon added, her dimples flashing as she smiled.

"And I'm Summer," Summer finished.

"This is my mama," Antonio said, and then turned to her. "These kind ladies helped me carry my things," he explained. "Luisa has just thrown them all out of her house."

Antonio's mum rolled her eyes at the girls. "That Luisa!" she cried, shaking her head. "She's always been one for dramatics!" She smiled at the girls. "It was kind of you to help my son. You must all come in and have a drink and something to eat. I insist!"

"Hey, Antonio!" came a voice, just then, from across the street.

Paige turned and saw a young man with dark curly hair striding towards them.

"Carlo!" Antonio cried. "What are you doing here?"

"I have good news," Carlo announced, with a nod to Antonio's mother and the girls. "The Count of Rome is holding a Christmas feast this evening, and he desperately needs a musician to play. I suggested . . . you!"

"*Me?*" repeated Antonio, looking dazed. "Me to play for the Count of Rome?"

"Yes, you," Carlo laughed. "You are to be at the house for seven o'clock. But, be warned, the Count is very hard to please. You must play all your best songs – including any Christmas songs you know. The Count loves carols."

Antonio beamed and clapped his friend on the shoulder. "Thank you, Carlo," he said delightedly. Then he picked up his mum, and twirled her around on the doorstep, making her shriek with laughter. Paige couldn't help smiling at his excitement. "This is my chance to show Luisa that I am a real musician!" Antonio cried. "Surely *this* will impress her!"

Antonio's mum looked very proud. "Fancy my son playing for the Count of Rome!" she marvelled. "Wonderful! Come in, all of you. Antonio, you must start practising at once!"

Chapter Seven

The girls followed Antonio into the front room of the house, where he asked them to make themselves comfortable. Antonio's mum brought through some bowls of vegetable soup and crusty bread for them to eat while they listened to him practise.

Antonio began plucking the strings of the mandolin, and singing a lovely, melodic song that Paige didn't recognize. *He's good*, she thought, sipping the warming soup as she listened.

He played a second song, and a third. Then Paige suddenly remembered what Carlo had said about the Count's love of Christmas songs. "Which Christmas carols are you going to play?" she asked, once Antonio had finished his third song.

Antonio listed a few carols, and then grimaced. "The thing is, they are not very interesting," he said. "I think I need something different . . ." He gazed thoughtfully at the pile of sheet music beside him and began searching through the pages. "I have been writing my own Christmas carol, but it is not yet finished," he told the girls.

"Could we hear it?" Shannon asked at once. "I love Christmas songs."

Antonio hesitated. "I have never played it to anyone before," he admitted. "And it isn't quite ready, but . . ." He nodded. "Yes, I will sing what I have written so far. It is called *Angel of Christmas Night*."

He placed his fingers on the mandolin strings once more, and began to sing and play his new song. Paige was entranced. She had never heard such a beautiful melody.

"Angel of Christmas Night
With wings of purest white . . ."

"Oh, that was *wonderful*," Summer sighed when he'd finished.

"It's a gorgeous tune," Shannon added. "You've *got* to play that one for the Count. It's brilliant!"

Antonio flushed with pleasure. "Do you think so? But I don't think there will be time to finish it now. I will have to leave soon," he said.

"Well . . . *I* like to sing," Shannon said hesitantly.

She sounded shyer than Paige had ever heard her. "Maybe . . . I could help?"

"We could all help," Summer suggested.

"Or at least try!" Paige put in eagerly.

Antonio beamed. "Thank you," he said. "Let's get to work!"

Within the hour, working as a team, the four of them had added a whole new verse to the song, and Shannon had helped develop the harmony. "There's just time for one more practice before I have to go," Antonio declared, looking excited. He sang the entire song through again for the girls and his mother.

Paige felt goose-pimply as she listened. Antonio's voice was pure and clear, and the melody was truly beautiful. There was a round of applause as he finished.

"Brilliant," Paige exclaimed. "Absolutely brilliant!"

Antonio's mother dabbed at her eyes with her apron and then flung her arms around her son and kissed the top of his head. "My son – he is a genius!" she declared.

Antonio grinned as he hugged his mum in return. "Thank you," he said. "But, Mama, these girls are geniuses too, you know." He slung his mandolin over his shoulder. "I must go now. Wish me luck, won't you? If my performance goes well, and Luisa gets to hear of it, it might just be a way to soften her heart!"

"Girls, will you stay here while Antonio is out?" Antonio's mum asked Paige, Summer and Shannon. "I would enjoy the company – unless you have somewhere else you need to be, of course."

"Thank you," Shannon said.

"We'd love to stay," Summer put in.

"We all want to know how Antonio gets on," Paige said with a smile. *And we don't exactly have anywhere else to go*, she thought. *Not until Velvet turns up again, anyway*. And Paige had a feeling that that wouldn't happen until they had solved the mystery of the Mona Lisa's smile.

Antonio's mother stoked up the fire in the living room, and lit some candles. "Have some hot milk," she said, passing cups around. "It will keep us all warm."

Paige sipped the hot drink and chatted happily

with her friends and Antonio's mother while they waited for Antonio's return. After an hour or two the door swung open and he bounded in.

"They loved it! They loved it!" he cried joyfully. *"Angel of Christmas Night* went like a dream. The Count demanded that I play it three times!"

"Oh, Antonio!" his mum cried in delight. "Well done!"

"That's fab!" Shannon cheered, jumping to her feet.

"We knew they'd love it!" Paige added, smiling.

"Well done!" Summer chimed in.

Antonio beamed. "And then, even better," he said, "the Count asked me if I would be his official court musician! Me! Antonio! It is my dream come true!"

"Oh, son," his mother clucked, rushing over to embrace him. "I am so proud!"

Antonio did a mock bow to the girls. "Paige, Summer and Shannon, you all helped me so much," he said. "Thank you. I couldn't have finished the song without you."

Shannon shook her head, smiling. "You would have got there in the end," she told him. "All we did was hurry things along a bit!"

"How did you come up with *Angel of Christmas Night* in the first place?" Summer asked with interest. "Have you written many songs before?"

"Yes, lots of songs," Antonio replied. "Sometimes a melody just comes to me," he explained. "I never set out to write a song – they just seem to find me."

"Well, you'll be writing lots more now that you're court musician," Shannon pointed out.

Paige gasped as a brilliant idea popped into her head. "Maybe you could write one for Luisa!" she suggested excitedly. "That could be the perfect birthday present to win her back!"

Antonio's eyes widened as he thought about it, and then his face lit up. He flung his arms around Paige. "It is a great idea! Bravo, Paige!" he cried. "A tune has been stuck in my head for the last few days – now I know that it *has* to be a love song! I will start work on it at once!"

Antonio sat by the fire with his mandolin, scribbling down words and humming a melody. Paige, Summer and Shannon helped for a little while, but soon Paige began to feel her eyelids droop, and she glanced at her friends to see that they were already fast asleep.

Antonio's mother wrapped some thick blankets round Summer and Shannon, and handed another to Paige. Paige smiled to herself as she curled up under her blanket, close to the fire, and closed her eyes. It was nice, falling asleep to the sweet notes of the mandolin, she thought drowsily, as she drifted off to sleep.

Chapter Eight

The next morning, the girls awoke to find Antonio looking bleary-eyed and rather dishevelled – but very pleased with himself.

"The song for my sweet Lisa is finished," he declared happily. "I am going to serenade her at once!"

Paige, Shannon and Summer wriggled out from underneath their blankets and leaped up. Paige could see that her friends were as excited at this news as she was.

"We'll come with you," Shannon said, grinning at Antonio. "Let's go!"

The cobbled streets were quiet in the morning sunlight. Most of the window shutters were still closed, but others had been flung open to let in the cool morning air. Birds sang, and the delicious smell of fresh bread floated from a little bakery they passed. A cat rolled in the dust at the side of the road, and Paige was reminded of Velvet, and wondered where she was and what she was doing.

"This is her house," Antonio said, staring up at the balcony. Then he sighed, looking despondent. "But the balcony doors are shut! How will Luisa hear me sing?"

"Maybe Paige, Summer and I could try and get into the house to see her," Shannon suggested. "Then, with any luck, we can persuade her to open the doors."

"Yes, that's a good idea," Summer said, and Antonio looked hopeful.

Paige smiled at him. "We'll take care of the balcony doors. You just start singing as soon as you see them open."

Antonio thanked the girls, his eyes still on the balcony. It was almost as if he were willing Luisa to step outside and see him there.

Meanwhile, the girls raced round to the front of the house and knocked at the door. As they stood on the front steps, waiting for someone to answer the door, a familiar black shape appeared in front of them: Velvet!

"There you are!" Paige cried, bending down to stroke her. "I was wondering where you were."

Summer grinned and bent down to stroke the kitten as well. "I'm glad you're back, Velvet."

"Me, too!" Shannon said, tickling Velvet under her chin.

Velvet stood on her back legs and scrabbled at the door. Paige laughed. "I think Velvet wants to get inside as much as we do!" she said.

Velvet miaowed and looked up at them all, her golden eyes very bright.

At that moment, a maid opened the door. "Yes?" she asked, looking curiously at the three girls and the kitten.

"We have a message for Lady Luisa," Shannon said. "May we come in?"

The maid shook her head. "I'm afraid that Lady Luisa is busy," she said firmly. "She can't be disturbed. Signor Leonardo has arrived early today to make up for yesterday's interruptions."

Paige tried a different tack. "Well then, I wonder if you could give Luisa a message from Antonio," she began, but at the mention of Antonio's name the maid narrowed her eyes and began to close the door. "Please," Paige said quickly. "He really needs Luisa to open the balcony doors," she begged. "He has something urgent to say to her."

The maid shook her head stubbornly. "Lady Luisa cannot be disturbed," she repeated snootily with her nose in the air.

As Paige looked down at her feet despondently, she glimpsed a flash of black whisk inside the house. She had to bite her lip to stop herself from laughing. The maid was so busy being snooty, she hadn't noticed Velvet slipping past her through the doorway. Paige managed to stifle a cheer as she saw Velvet race up the stairs behind the maid and tried desperately to think of a way that they could follow the kitten.

But just then Summer let out a big sigh of defeat and turned away, as if she were about to leave. Then, all of a sudden, she dodged to the left of the maid – and raced straight past her, into the house!

Paige gaped at Shannon in surprise. Had shy Summer *really* just run into a stranger's house without permission?

Shannon shrugged and grinned, and, before the maid could gather her wits, she and Paige both dashed past the maid after Velvet and Summer.

"Hey!" called the maid. "Come back! You can't just go barging in there!"

Too late! Paige thought as she followed Summer and Velvet up the stairs and into a large, bright room. *We just did!*

As Paige ran into the room, she saw Luisa sitting in a chair by the window.

Leonardo da Vinci was standing before his easel, his brush poised in mid-air, as he turned to see what the noise was. "What in heaven's name—" he began, but Paige and her friends rushed past him and over to Luisa.

"Lady Luisa," Summer was saying breathlessly, "there's something you really need to hear."

Paige noticed that Velvet was pawing at the balcony doors, and she ran over to open them. Shannon joined her, and the two girls pulled back the balcony doors together. Almost instantly, the strains of a beautiful song floated up through the window and everyone stopped talking to listen.

"I'm sorry, ma'am," the maid panted, bursting into the room just then. "I tried to stop them, but—"

Luisa held up her hand for silence. "Quiet,

Maria. All is well," she said, a faraway look on her face. "And this song is *beautiful!*"

The song *was* beautiful, Paige agreed silently. The tune was simple but enchanting, and Antonio's words were tender and romantic. Luisa looked utterly bewitched.

Paige noticed that Leonardo da Vinci was watching Luisa too, and as she smiled at the love song he grabbed his pencil and began to sketch furiously. "That smile is perfect! Hold it right there!" he cried, his pencil flying across the canvas.

But Luisa was getting to her feet. "I'm sorry, Leonardo, but I have to go," she told the artist, and she ran out on to the balcony.

"Antonio! It is the most wonderful song I have ever heard!" Paige heard her cry. "Wait there!" And then Luisa re-entered the room, and dashed downstairs without a backward glance, her maid hurrying after her.

Paige glanced over at Leonardo da Vinci, feeling somewhat guilty for interrupting his painting. "Um . . . We're sorry about that," she began, "but we . . ."

The artist looked up briefly from his easel.

"Silence! I insist!" he murmured, his face a picture of concentration. "Lisa's smile was perfect. It spoke a thousand words. I must sketch it before my memory fades. Leave me to my work!"

Paige heard a miaow from the balcony, and ran outside to join Velvet. The little cat was peeping through the iron railings, and Paige and her friends looked down curiously, just in time to see Luisa throwing herself into Antonio's arms.

The girls grinned at one another.

"I just *love* a happy ending," Summer sighed.

A thought struck Paige. "So *that's* why Luisa's smiling in the portrait," she declared. "It was because she'd just heard Antonio's song!"

"Fantastic!" exclaimed Shannon. "What a story this will make for our English project!"

Paige grinned and bent down to pick up Velvet. "Thank you for our adventure, Velvet," she said, cuddling the kitten gently.

"Yes, it's been great," Summer agreed, stroking Velvet's head.

Velvet looked up at the three girls, and her whiskers began to shimmer.

"I think we're about to go home," Shannon

said, seeing the golden glimmer.

"Goodbye, Antonio, goodbye, Luisa!" Paige shouted down to the couple below.

"We're going now," Summer called.

"Good luck!" shouted Shannon.

Antonio and Luisa waved to the girls before turning and walking down the street together, arm in arm. Then everything blurred before Paige's eyes, and she held on to Velvet tightly as the world seemed to spin around her.

Seconds later, the girls were back in the snowy herb garden of Charm Hall School.

"Wow!" Paige said, looking around at the falling snow. "Did all of that really happen?"

"It sure did!" Shannon declared happily. "I've still got Antonio's songs going round in my head."

"Same here," Summer agreed. She looked down at her watch. "And according to this, we've only been gone a couple of minutes!"

Paige glanced at her own watch, and realized that Velvet was no longer in her arms. "Come on, let's go back to the dorm," she said. "I hope Velvet's there. She's going to get so many cuddles!"

Chapter Nine

Dear Mum and Dad, Paige typed in the computer room a few weeks later.

I've got lots to tell you! School's been really busy, with everyone getting ready for Christmas. Shannon, Summer and I have been working really hard (honest!) on a *Mona Lisa* project. We wrote a story about the *Mona Lisa*'s smile (I'll show it to you in the Christmas holidays) and painted a modern version of the picture in art. And guess what? We each got an A – top marks!

I've been making prezzies for my friends here too, to go in their Christmas stockings. (It's a tradition here.) I painted some picture frames and have glued beads around them, and I'm going to draw some funny pictures of Summer, Shannon and me to go inside them.

Shannon's parents sent us some decorations, so our dorm is looking really pretty at the moment. And everyone's excited about the Christmas carol competition. Did I tell you that Shannon's in the choir? She's been practising loads, and gets Summer and me to sing along with her in the dorm so that she can learn all the words. The competition is just around the corner now. Of course we all want Charm Hall Choir to win.

That's all for now – better go. Love you loads. Write soon, Paige xxx

Paige smiled as she sent the email and then closed down the computer. She enjoyed herself too much at school to get *really* homesick, but every now and then, when she read their emails or spoke to them on the phone, she missed her parents. But it was only a few days now until the end of term, and then she was going to spend three whole weeks with them over Christmas. She could hardly wait!

"Ah, Paige," came a voice as she left

the computer room. "Would you run an errand for me, please?"

Paige looked up to see Miss Linnet heading towards her. The head was clutching a folded piece of paper and looking rather flustered, which was very unusual.

"Of course," Paige replied.

"It's very important," Miss Linnet went on. "I've just received the official list of songs that each school will be performing in the carol competition, and unfortunately Woodlands School has chosen the exact same three carols as we have." She pressed the piece of paper into Paige's hand. "I've got to go to a meeting now, so would you take this message to Miss Montgomery at once, please? I want her to read it as soon as possible."

"Sure," Paige said. "I'll go right now."

Paige turned and raced towards the music room. On the way she bumped into Summer, who was coming back from gym practice. When Paige told her what had happened, Summer decided to go with her to deliver the message.

The girls soon reached the music room, and Paige handed the note to Miss Montgomery. The music teacher read it and sighed. "How very unfortunate," she murmured. Then she turned to address the choir. "Girls, I'm very sorry, but we're going to have to change one of our carols. I know it's short notice, but Woodlands School has chosen the same three, and we don't want our programmes to be the same."

"Is there enough time to practise another carol?" one of the Year Seven girls, Laura, asked in dismay. "The competition's tomorrow!"

"I know, but . . ." Miss Montgomery ran a hand through her hair, looking anxious. "We need something that will make us stand out. Think, everybody. What carol can we sing to show that Charm Hall School is special?"

"Excuse me, Miss Montgomery," Summer said, blushing. "But I know the perfect carol – and Shannon can teach it to you all."

Shannon looked confused for a moment, and then her face cleared. "Oh, you mean *Angel of Christmas Night*. Good thinking, Summer!"

"*Angel of Christmas Night*?" Miss Montgomery echoed. "I don't think I know that one."

"Our friend Antonio wrote it," Shannon

explained with a proud grin. "It goes like this . . ." And without another word she launched into the carol and everyone else fell silent.

"Angel of Christmas Night,
With wings of purest white . . ."

Paige listened, smiling. She'd forgotten what a lovely song it was – and Shannon really did it justice with her beautiful voice.

When Shannon finished singing, everyone started clapping and talking excitedly.

"I *love* it!" cried Holly.

"Where did you say you learned it?" Sophie wanted to know.

"Can we sing it in the competition, Miss Montgomery? Can we sing *Angel of Christmas Night*?" asked Serena and Sasha.

Miss Montgomery was smiling too. "Thank you, Shannon. I think we've just found our new carol!" she said. "Could you sing it for us again, please? I'll start working out the chords on the piano to accompany you."

Shannon sang the carol for a second time, and Paige chalked up the words on the blackboard so that everyone could see them. By the time Shannon got to the last chorus, the whole choir was singing along.

Miss Montgomery looked jubilant. "Girls, that sounded wonderful!" she cried. "Now, let's have a think about harmonies . . ."

Paige and Summer stayed to watch the rehearsal. It took a while, but the choir eventually mastered the harmonies and learned the words.

"Lovely," Miss Montgomery said as they sang it all the way through one last time. "Absolutely lovely. But do you know, it's such a gorgeous and unusual song, I almost feel it needs something extra – something visual – just as the finishing touch. I wonder if . . ." She shook her head. "No. We don't have time to make costumes now. I'll have to think of something else. In the meantime, keep practising and I'll see you all tomorrow."

Paige, Shannon and Summer walked upstairs to their dorm, all humming *Angel of Christmas Night*.

"Oh, Velvet," Shannon said in amusement, as they entered their room. "Have you been playing with our decorations again?"

Paige laughed to see that Velvet had knocked an

angel-shaped bauble off the door handle and was playing with it on the floor.

Suddenly, Shannon clapped her hands in excitement. "Hey!" she said excitedly. "I've just thought. Since the new carol is *Angel of Christmas Night*, why don't we have someone dressed up as an angel on stage with us?"

"Ooh, that would look lovely!" Summer cried.

"Brilliant!" Paige agreed. "She could carry a candle. That would look really Christmassy."

Shannon nodded eagerly. "And what if everyone in the choir has a candle too – an unlit one, I mean. Then the angel can come along with her candle and light everyone else's!"

All the girls grinned at each other. "Perfect," Summer said. "Everyone will love it!"

"Now we just need to find an angel," Paige said. Then she laughed suddenly as an idea struck her. "Hey! I know just the right person – Lily!"

Chapter Ten

"Oh, yes, of course!" Shannon exclaimed. "Let's go and see Miss Montgomery right now and ask her what she thinks."

"Sorry, Velvet," Summer said, making for the door. "We're off again. We've got a plan to put into action!"

Paige bent down to stroke the kitten, and picked up the angel bauble. "I almost think you were playing with this on purpose, Miss Velvet," she smiled. "To put the idea into our heads!"

The girls ran back down to the music room, where Miss Montgomery was playing *Angel of*

Christmas Night and writing down chords. "Hello again," she said. "Goodness, you all look very excited. What's going on?"

Shannon explained their idea, and the music teacher's eyes sparkled. "I like it," she said approvingly. "Do you think Lily will want to be our angel?"

"Yes," the girls chorused.

"She was supposed to be the angel in her school nativity play," Paige explained. "And she was really disappointed when she couldn't do it any more."

"We'll go and ask her," Shannon said. "Back in ten minutes, Miss Montgomery!"

The girls ran over to Sam's cottage to find Lily. She and Sam had been making mince pies, and they were both laughing and covered in icing sugar.

"Lily, we've had an idea!" Paige said, as Sam welcomed them into the warm kitchen.

"It's about the carol concert," Shannon went on, grinning. "We need a special helper, to be our angel. And we were wondering . . ."

"If *you'd* like to do it!" Summer finished, the words tumbling out.

Paige smiled at the little girl. She just knew Lily

would love the idea of being an angel! But to Paige's surprise Lily looked back at the girls with solemn eyes . . . and then shook her head.

"I can't be the angel," she said.

"What do you mean, you can't?" Shannon asked, looking mystified.

"Is it that you don't *want* to be?" Summer queried.

"I *do* want to!" Lily cried. "But I didn't bring my wings with me. They're still at home."

Sam chuckled and gave Lily a big hug. "Wings? We can make you some *wings*!" he said. "Don't let that stop you being the angel!"

Lily looked up at her grandpa as if he were a superhero. "Really? You can *make* wings?" she asked.

Sam nodded. "I certainly can!" he replied. "We'll need some wire to make the frame, but I've got loads of that. And we'll need some sort of sparkly material too . . . Ah." He stopped. "I don't have anything like that in the cottage. What could we use?"

"There might be some in the textiles room," Shannon suggested. "We'll ask if we can have a look."

"Yes, and, Lily, you could come and choose some

with us," Paige suggested, holding out her hand. "If that's all right, Sam?"

He nodded. "Of course," he said. "I'll get your coat. Make sure you pick out something really special!"

Lily skipped for joy as they walked over to the school.

Miss Montgomery was waiting for them. "Well? Are you going to be our Christmas angel?" she asked Lily with a smile.

Lily nodded shyly. "Yes, please," she said.

"Fantastic!" Miss Montgomery exclaimed. "Thank you!"

"Can we get some material for some angel wings, Miss Montgomery?" Paige asked. "Sam says he'll make them for Lily."

"Of course," the teacher said. "I'm sure Mrs Harper won't mind at all. I'll unlock the textiles room for you."

A few minutes later, they all trooped into the textiles room. The girls instantly made for the five large material bins standing at the back of the classroom.

"I need to finish printing the song sheets for our new carol," Miss Montgomery said, "but I'll come back and see how you're getting on as soon as I've done that. Happy hunting!" She closed the door and the girls grinned at each other.

"Angel material, here we come!" Shannon said, diving into the first bin. She held up a strip of grey flannel, wrinkling her nose. "But this won't do! You'll look like the *elephant* of Christmas night if we dress you in this!"

"Hmmm, I wonder if Antonio ever thought of that one?" Summer giggled. She started to sing:

"Elephant of Christmas Day
With your trunk of purest grey . . ."

Paige burst out laughing. "Summer! If only you'd thought of that earlier, Antonio could have sung it to the—" She broke off as she noticed Lily's curious look.

"Who's Antonio?" the younger girl asked.

"Um . . . He's just a friend," Paige replied, busying herself by looking into another material bin.

"Ooh, how about this?" Shannon said a few minutes later. She draped a piece of silky fuchsia material around her shoulders and tilted her head, trying to assume an angelic expression. "Do I look like a pink angel?"

"A pink disco diva, more like!" Paige laughed.

"Angels wear *white*," Lily said firmly.

"She's right," Summer agreed. " 'Wings of purest white'; even the words say so, remember?"

The girls went on looking. There was lots of beige cotton in Paige's bin, and some navy-blue corduroy, but nothing very sparkly or glitzy. And none of it was delicate enough for angel wings.

The others weren't having much luck either.

"Well, this is white," Summer said, sounding rather defeated as she held up some plain cotton. "But it's not very pretty."

"There must be *some*thing better," Paige said.

Lily nodded, a determined glint in her eye. " 'Find something special', Grandpa Sam said. We've *got* to keep looking!"

Chapter Eleven

Paige smiled at the determination on Lily's face. Now that she had been given a second chance at being an angel, it seemed the little girl wasn't going to let it slip away.

Just then, Paige felt something brush against her legs. She looked down to see Velvet slinking past, keeping herself flat against the material bin, almost as if she didn't want to be seen. Paige watched as Velvet slipped through the gap between Paige's bin and Lily's, wondering what the kitten was up to.

Something magical, I bet, Paige thought. *I'd better get Lily out of here so that she doesn't see it!*

"Lily, there's a storeroom over there," Paige said quickly, pointing to a door in the far wall. "Would you mind having a look in there? There might be some better material inside."

"OK," Lily replied, straightening up and heading over to it.

As soon as she'd gone, Velvet emerged from her hiding place.

"Shannon, Summer," Paige said in a low voice, pointing down at the kitten. "Look who's here."

"Oh, good!" Summer exclaimed happily. "Have you come to help, Velvet?"

Velvet closed her eyes, then flicked her tail back and forth. Her whiskers shimmered golden, and Paige gasped as the fabrics from the textile bins flew up in the air and whirled around together, surrounded by a cloud of sparkling golden stars. Paige felt her mouth fall open as she watched the tiny glittering stars swirl all over the fabrics as they tumbled around in mid-air. It was a bit like watching fireworks.

"I can't find anything good in here," Paige heard Lily call from the store cupboard.

And at that moment all the fabrics fell from

the air, down into the bins once more.

Lily came out of the storeroom, a disappointed look on her face, and Paige shut her mouth with a snap, and tried to look as if nothing amazing had just happened.

Velvet chose that moment to jump on to the edge of one of the fabric bins and balance there.

"Oh, it's the kitten! Hello, Velvet!" Lily cried, rushing over to pet her.

Velvet jumped right into the bin, as if she

was playing hide-and-seek, and Lily leaned over to search among the fabrics, laughing. "She's so sweet," she said. "Come on, kitty. I'll help you out of the— Oh!"

"What is it?" Summer asked.

Lily emerged from the bin, clutching a piece of material and looking overjoyed. "Look what I've found! We could make angel wings out of *this*!"

Lily was holding up a piece of beautiful white silk, which was shot through with silver stars. "It's *perfect!*" she breathed.

Velvet leaped out of the bin, purring, and Paige saw that the kitten had been sitting on another piece of the same glittering fabric.

"Hey," Paige said, reaching in and pulling out the cloth. "There's this bit too."

Lily was hugging the first piece of silk, her eyes sparkling with happiness. "I just can't believe I didn't see this stuff before!" she cried.

"You know, I think there might be enough material here to make a dress as well as wings," Paige said, unfolding the second piece of silk quickly in an attempt to distract Lily. "What do you think, Lil?"

Lily grinned. "Ooh, yes, *please!*" she said.

Velvet immediately headed for the door, mewing to be let out. Paige opened it for her and watched the little cat slip away around the corner – just seconds before Miss Montgomery came along the corridor.

"How are you getting on, girls?" the teacher asked. "Have you found anything suitable?"

Paige smiled. "Yes," she said. "We were just wondering whether we could use it for a dress as well as wings."

Miss Montgomery examined the material. "It's beautiful," she said. "And a dress *would* be nice. I wonder if Mia could help us. She did such a good job making the costumes for the school play, didn't she?"

"Good idea," Shannon said. "How about I take some of this material to Sam, so that he can make a start on the wings, while you guys go and talk to Mia?"

Paige nodded. "We'll meet you in Mia's room in a few minutes."

Paige, Summer and Lily went up to find Mia, who shared a room with Abigail and Chloe. Paige

92

really hoped Abigail wouldn't be around. Abigail was bound to make some kind of annoying comment if she was.

Luckily Mia was alone in the dorm, and happy to help Lily. "Of course I will!" she said. "I'll just get my tape measure out, and then we can start."

Mia took Lily's measurements and began cutting the silk to size. Paige started to feel excited. The plan was coming together brilliantly!

Lily looked excited too. She was hopping from foot to foot and talking non-stop about the carol concert.

Paige and Summer were just helping Mia pin up the hem when Shannon arrived.

"Ooh, it's looking good," Shannon said, winking at Lily. "*Angel of Christmas Night . . .*" she sang. "*It's Lily in shimmering white . . .*"

Just then Abigail came into the room. "What are you lot doing in here?" she demanded in her usual rude way.

Summer raised her eyes from the piece of silk she was pinning. "Mia's helping us make a dress for Lily," she replied. "Lily's going to be an angel in the carol competition."

"An angel? What a stupid idea!" Abigail snapped.

Shannon opened her mouth to reply, but Lily beat her to it.

"It's *not* a stupid idea," she said, with her hands on her hips and a fierce look on her face. "It's a *great* idea. Even the teacher said so. I'm going to be the best angel ever, and Charm Hall Choir is going to *win*, so there!"

Abigail looked a bit taken aback at this outburst, but everyone else in the room burst into cheers.

"Well said, Lily!" Shannon declared, unable to hide her grin.

Mia looked up from the hem of the dress and smiled. Then she glanced at Abigail. "Well, are you going to give us a hand with this dress? Or are you going to stand there scowling all day?" she asked.

Looking uncharacteristically shamefaced, Abigail shrugged. "I could help a bit, I suppose," she muttered.

"Good," said Mia getting up and dumping a length of silk in Abigail's arms. "You can pin up this sleeve for me. Now, let's get this show on the road!"

Chapter Twelve

"Silent night, holy night
 All is calm, all is bright . . ."

Paige drank in the sound of the Charm Hall Choir singing on stage. She was standing just a few metres away, waiting in the wings with Summer and Lily.

They were all at the Churchill School's theatre, and Paige and Summer had been allowed backstage to look after Lily and help her get ready for her big moment.

Paige couldn't resist peeping around the red velvet stage curtain to see Shannon and the rest of the choir singing their hearts out. Summer and Lily were watching too.

The Charm Hall girls are doing really well, Paige thought to herself. But the other choirs had been great too. It was going to be difficult for the judges to choose the winning school.

Paige stepped away from the curtain. "Lily, we'd better get your wings on," she said quietly. "They're going to sing *Angel of Christmas Night* next."

"OK," said Lily, looking excited and nervous at the same time.

"You'll be great," Summer assured her, carefully attaching the first wing to the Velcro strips Mia had sewn into the back of the angel dress.

Meanwhile Paige knelt down to hand Lily a fat white church candle, which the little girl held firmly in both hands.

Miss Montgomery came over and gave Lily a hug, before lighting the candle for her. "Be very careful with the candle, won't you?" she reminded Lily. "Hold it really still, just like we practised."

"I will, Miss Montgomery," Lily said solemnly.

Paige put the second wing in place. "There," she said. "I've never seen a prettier angel!"

"*Silent Night* is just finishing," Summer whispered, hearing the last notes dying away. "This is it, Lily – you're on!"

Lily's eyes looked enormous, and Paige could see the bright flame of the candle reflected in them. "I'm excited," she said confidingly to Paige.

"Good luck," Paige smiled. "Enjoy it!"

She and Summer watched Lily walk on stage with her candle. The audience gave a gasp of surprise and delight.

"Come on," Paige said, grabbing Summer's hand. "Let's go and watch with the rest of the audience."

The two girls ran quietly round to the back of the stalls and slipped into a couple of empty seats. There was a hush as Shannon started the carol with a solo line, and Paige felt goosebumps prickling up her arms as she listened to her friend's clear voice.

"I don't know this one," someone nearby whispered, and Paige saw a woman checking her programme. "It's called *Angel of Christmas Night*. Isn't it lovely?"

"Oh, look, how sweet," the woman next to her murmured, as Lily advanced along the front row of the choir, lighting candles.

"Gorgeous!" someone else breathed.

Paige couldn't help grinning. It was all going perfectly. Lily looked adorable in her angel outfit, and with all the candles alight the scene really did look like something from a Christmas card.

At the end of the carol, there was a moment's silence, and then the audience erupted with a round of thunderous applause. A couple of people even cheered and whistled! The choir members, all grinning, blew out their candles, and Paige clapped as hard as she could.

"None of the other songs got cheers like this!" Summer commented, her eyes shining as she clapped furiously.

"Oh, weren't they brilliant?" Paige said happily, as the Charm Hall girls walked off stage. "And didn't Lily look sweet?"

Summer nodded and grinned. "Let's go and see her," she said, and she and Paige made their way backstage again to find Lily. But someone had beaten them to it. Lily was being hugged by Sam, while a smiling couple looked on, telling her how wonderful she'd been.

"Thanks, Mum. Thanks, Dad!" Lily said, going over to give them a hug too. "I didn't know you were going to be here!"

Paige felt a lump in her throat at the sight. She'd never seen Lily look so happy.

"Shannon!" Summer exclaimed suddenly, as their friend came up. "You were brilliant! All the carols sounded fantastic, especially *Angel of Christmas Night.*"

The three friends hugged each other. "I just hope it was good enough to win," Shannon said nervously. "I thought all the other schools sang really well too."

Paige glanced over at Lily's family to see the little girl up on her granddad's shoulders, and Lily's parents holding hands. Paige smiled, feeling really pleased for her friend, and secretly hoping that Lily might be home for a happy family Christmas.

The girls waited nervously together for the judges' decision.

"I've already bitten all my nails off," Shannon moaned after a little while. "What's taking them so long? I wish they'd just—"

She was interrupted by a voice from the stage. "Ladies and gentlemen, the judges' results are in, and I will now announce the winners of this year's School Choir Carol Competition."

The girls peeped around the curtain to see the head judge standing on stage.

"In third place . . ." she said, ". . . Woodlands School."

The Woodlands Choir filed on stage to an enthusiastic round of applause. The judge motioned to them to stand on the left of the stage.

"In second place . . ." the judge continued, ". . . Draycott Comprehensive."

Again, the audience applauded as the choir marched onstage eagerly. Then they took their places to the left of the judge.

The judge smiled into the audience. "It's my very great pleasure to announce that this year's winning choir is . . ."

She paused dramatically and Paige crossed all her fingers.

"Charm Hall!" the judge declared.

The hall erupted with applause, and, backstage, all the Charm Hall girls danced around cheering until Miss Montgomery ushered them out onstage, to even louder clapping.

"Come on, Lily, you too," Miss Montgomery smiled.

Sam swung Lily down from his shoulders and she ran over excitedly to join the others onstage.

"Well done, girls," the judge said, presenting the trophy – a shining golden cup – to Holly, the oldest member of the choir. Holly thanked her, then passed it to Lily, who lifted it as high as she could, looking thrilled.

"Yay!" cheered Paige and Summer from the wings. "Go, Charm Hall!"

By the time the Charm Hall girls arrived back at school, Lily had fallen asleep, and Sam had to carry her off the minibus.

"She's going back home tomorrow," Sam told the girls. "Her parents have sorted out their problems, and I think everything's going to be all right."

"That's great news, Sam!" Paige exclaimed, and Shannon and Summer grinned.

Sam smiled. "Thank you so much for helping Lily settle in here, girls, and for the stocking full of presents too. That was very kind of you all."

Paige glanced at Shannon and Summer, feeling confused. *Presents? Stocking?* she wondered.

Sam winked. He seemed to think that they were being secretive, rather than just completely bemused. "I'm not sure how you managed to sneak it on to the end of her bed like that," he went on. "And the note was a lovely touch – 'to the Angel of the Carol Night' – so sweet! I can tell you, she's going to be really chuffed when she sees what you've done!"

Paige was just about to say that she didn't know what Sam was talking about, when she heard a little miaow, and saw Velvet winding around Summer's ankles. She grinned at her friends, suddenly guessing *exactly* who was responsible for Lily's stocking – Velvet, of course!

"Happy holidays, anyway," Sam was saying. "And I'll see you next term." He glanced down at Lily. "I'd better get this one tucked up in bed. Goodnight!"

"Come along, girls," Miss Montgomery called, sticking her head out of the school doorway. "It's late. You need to get ready for bed now." And then she withdrew into the entrance hall again.

Paige and her friends hurried towards school, with Velvet racing along in the shadows beside them. "It *was* you, wasn't it, Velvet?" Summer said in a whisper, stopping at the door to stroke Velvet. "A stocking for Lily – what a great idea!"

"You *are* fabulous," Shannon agreed, crouching down to pet the kitten. "The most magical cat ever!"

Paige bent down to give Velvet one last cuddle before going into the school. "We'll see you back at the dorm," she whispered. Then she kissed the kitten's little head, and heard her rumbling with purrs. "Thank you," she added, "for making this the most exciting and magical Christmas term I've ever had!"

If you want to read more

about the magic at

Charm Hall, then

turn over for the start of

the next adventure ...

Chapter One

Paige Hart shaded her eyes from the sun and gazed out across the jousting arena. A thrill of excitement shot through her. She could see two knights in glittering silver armour moving slowly across the field on horseback. The knights wore tunics over their armour, one red, the other midnight blue, and they carried matching shields emblazoned with gold lions.

Paige whirled round and scanned the crowd for her best friends Summer and Shannon. She saw them watching a puppet show just a little way off, and dashed over to them.

"The jousting contest's about to start," Paige said breathlessly.

"Oh, we can't miss *that*!" Shannon exclaimed. "Come on!" And lifting the hem of her flowing dress she dashed off towards the jousting arena, with Paige and Summer right behind her. As they ran, Paige couldn't help laughing to see that Shannon was wearing her trainers under her medieval dress.

Paige had been at Charm Hall Boarding School long enough now to know that there was always something exciting going on. This Sunday it was medieval pageant day. Miss Linnet, their headteacher, had explained in assembly earlier in the week that the medieval pageant day was held annually in the spring to celebrate the medieval origins of Charm Hall. As Paige, Summer and Shannon were in their first year at Charm Hall, this was their first time at the pageant. Along with the other pupils and teachers, Paige had really enjoyed dressing up in medieval clothes, and she was pleased to see that lots of people who had been invited from the nearby village had dressed up too. The trees were hung with colourful embroidered banners and flags, there were exciting activities like the jousting contest and there were lots of stalls selling medieval food and goods too.

"It really *is* like being back in medieval times," Paige said to Summer and Shannon, as they wove their way through the crowd to the jousting arena.

"It's hard work running in a long dress, though, isn't it?" Summer commented as they reached the edge of the arena.

Shannon nodded. "Especially with all these people about," she added. "I'm glad I put my trainers on!"

Summer pointed at the ring. "Look, they're about to start."

A page stepped forward into the middle of the arena and sounded a fanfare on a trumpet. "Welcome, good citizens, to the Charm Hall jousting contest," the page proclaimed, lowering the trumpet. "Our first two contestants are the Red Knight and the Blue Knight!"

The two knights lifted their visors and waved at the crowd.

"Look, it's Sam!" Shannon cried in delight. "And Miss Drake!"

"Our caretaker versus our PE teacher!" Paige said

with a grin. "I wonder who's going to win?"

Cheers were echoing around the arena as the knights turned their horses to face each other. Then they lifted their shining silver lances and stared hard at each other, their horses pawing the ground impatiently.

"Those lances look pretty real, don't they?" Shannon remarked.

"Don't worry, they're made out of foam!" Summer said with a grin. "I helped Miss Drake carry them out to the sports field."

Paige was clapping along with everyone else when she suddenly spied a little black kitten that she and her friends had named Velvet. A stage had been set up at the side of the arena, and Miss Linnet the headmistress, the mayor, the local vicar and some of the other villagers were sitting there. Velvet was perched on the edge of the stage, watching the proceedings with interest.

"Look!" Paige pointed the kitten out to Summer and Shannon. "Velvet's sitting with the VIPs!"

"Well, Velvet *is* a Very Important Person," Summer replied with a smile. "Or a Very Important Kitten, anyway!"

"There's *nobody* at Charm Hall who's more important or special than Velvet," Shannon agreed firmly.

Paige nodded. Velvet had a lot to do with how exciting things always were at Charm Hall. The kitten had mysteriously appeared in the girls' dorm one wet afternoon, and they had realized very quickly that Velvet was no ordinary kitten. She was a witch cat with incredible magic powers that constantly amazed and delighted the three friends. The girls still didn't know much about Velvet at all, although they did know that the magical kitten was somehow closely connected with Charm Hall, where she came and went at will.

Miss Linnet, looking very different in her grand red gown, was now standing on the platform, a white flag in her hand. There was a burst of applause as she waved the flag high above her head.

Immediately the Red Knight and the Blue Knight urged their horses forward. They charged towards each other, the thunder of the horses' hooves echoing around the arena.

"Who do you think will win: Sam or Miss Drake?" Shannon yelled above the sound of the hooves and the cheers of the crowd.

"No idea!" Paige yelled back.

"I don't know either," Summer shouted. "Miss Drake is determined, but Sam looks pretty comfortable on that horse.'

The two knights had galloped alongside each other now. Their lances locked as each tried to knock the other's shield to the ground. After a brief tussle the Red Knight managed to sweep the Blue Knight's shield out of her grasp. It fell to the ground and the crowd broke into more applause.

"Sam's won!" Shannon laughed.

Paige cheered along with everyone else as the Red and Blue Knights took a bow, and exited the arena. When she glanced over to the stage again Paige saw that Velvet had vanished. Paige grinned to herself. None of them ever knew where the mysterious kitten was going to appear next!

"It's the Green Knight versus the Yellow Knight now," Summer announced, as two new contestants rode into the arena and lifted their visors. "Ooh, look, it's Mrs Stark against Miss Mackenzie!"

"Then I *definitely* want Miss Mackenzie to win!" Shannon said firmly.

"Me too," Paige agreed. Their form teacher was a whole lot nicer than bad-tempered Mrs Stark!

The girls watched nervously as the two teachers raced towards each other. But it was a clean win for Miss Mackenzie as her lance knocked Mrs Stark's shield to the ground. The girls cheered enthusiastically.

"That was brilliant!" Shannon announced fifteen minutes later, as the last two contestants took their bows and exited the arena.

Paige nodded and Summer grinned.

"Let's go and check out the stalls now," Summer suggested.

The girls wandered off towards the stalls. All sorts of medieval items were for sale, from pots of herbs to embroidered flags and banners.

"Oh, look!" Paige exclaimed, stopping at a stall that was covered with miniature paper scrolls. She opened one up and saw that it contained a short poem, beginning with a beautifully painted, large letter "T" outlined in gold. "Aren't these gorgeous?"

The girls' art teacher, Miss Arnold, was running the stall, and she smiled at them. "Have you seen pictures of illuminated medieval manuscripts, girls?"

she asked. "The writers used to make the first letter on the page very large and beautiful with lots of colour, and pictures too. You can buy a scroll with your initial on it, if you like."

"Oh, yes, please!" Shannon exclaimed, picking up a scroll which had an *S* painted on it in vivid green. A tiny black kitten sat next to the letter, its tail entwined in the curves of the *S*. "I'll have this – it reminds me of someone!" And she winked at the others. "Here's the same one for you, Summer." Paige grinned as she picked up a scroll with an elaborate illuminated *P* decorated with pink roses, green ivy leaves and two birds peeping out of the flowers.

"This is lovely, but I don't think I've got enough money on me," Paige sighed. She checked her purse and shook her head. "Nope, I'll have to go back to the dorm."

"I haven't got enough to lend you either," Shannon said, as she poked through the coins in her purse.

"Me neither," Summer sighed. "Sorry, Paige."

"Oh, those are lovely!" said a voice behind them. Paige looked round and saw Penny Harris, one of their friends, staring closely at the illuminated letters.

"Here, you can have this one!" Paige handed the *P* to Penny with a grin. "I haven't got enough money on me anyway."

"Oh, I can lend you some," Penny said kindly. She picked up another *P* and held them both out to Miss Arnold. "You can pay me back later, Paige."

"Oh, thanks, Pen," Paige said, giving her a grateful smile.

"No problem," Penny said, glancing at her watch. "I've got to go." And she hurried away.

"We'll see you in the archery demonstration later," Summer called after her, but Penny had already disappeared into the crowd.

"I'm getting hungry," Shannon remarked as they walked on. She looked longingly at the food stalls. "Honey cakes, fruit pies and hog roast," she read out. "They *all* sound delicious!"

"Hey, there's Velvet again," Summer said, pointing ahead of them. The little black kitten was weaving her way between the visitors' legs, stopping every so often to let someone stroke her.

It was lucky that there were several farms in the

countryside around the school, Paige thought, because everyone who saw Velvet always assumed that the kitten was one of the farm cats. Pets weren't allowed at Charm Hall, and the girls had to keep Velvet's presence in their dorm a closely guarded secret.

"Look at that little girl who's stroking Velvet!" Paige exclaimed. "It's Lily!"

"Let's go and say hello," Shannon suggested.

Lily was Sam the school caretaker's five-year-old granddaughter. She had stayed with Sam for a little while when her parents were having problems, but then everything had been sorted out and she'd gone back home.

"Hi, Lily!" Shannon said cheerfully. "Are you enjoying the pageant?"

Lily nodded. "I'm having a great time!" she replied, as Velvet began to purr loudly. "My mum and dad brought me." She pointed at a couple standing in the queue for the hog roast.

"Did you see the jousting, Lily?" asked Paige, bending down to scratch Velvet's ears. "Your granddad was great!"

"I know." Lily beamed happily. "We've just been

116

watching him. And we've been inside the school too, to see the really *old* bit of the building!"

"Ah, you mean the medieval part," said Summer, and Lily nodded. "Miss Linnet always opens up the medieval section of the school to the public on Pageant Day so that they can go and see it," Summer explained to Paige. "It's a tradition."

Paige looked interested. "That's the hallway near the school office, isn't it?" she asked. "The one near that funny little round tower?"

Shannon nodded. "The hallway and the tower are both medieval," she agreed. "And didn't Miss Mackenzie say that this year there's going to be a display of medieval objects that have been found around the school, as well?"

"Yes, we saw it," Lily chimed in. "And there's a *really* beautiful old dress which is *exactly* the same colour as Velvet's collar." And she pointed down at Velvet, who had stuck her head under the hem of Shannon's dress and was playing with her trainer laces.

Paige felt a thrill of excitement run through her. She had been around Velvet long enough to know that nothing was ever just a coincidence where the kitten was concerned! Was Velvet connected to the dress in some way? "Really?" she asked Lily as casually as she could, flicking a glance at Shannon and Summer. Her friends looked just as excited as she felt. "You're sure it was the *exact* same colour?"

Lily nodded and then turned her head, as someone called her name. "I've got to go. I'll see you later," she said, before running over to her parents who were carrying bread rolls filled with steaming hog roast.

"We've got to check this dress out!" Shannon said eagerly, as Velvet trotted eagerly after Lily, evidently attracted by the smell of Lily's lunch.

"Velvet looks hungry, and I thought you were too, Shannon," Summer teased.

"This is more important," Shannon declared. "We might be able to find out something more about Velvet!"

"Let's go," Paige agreed.

Picking up their skirts, the three girls hurried through the crowd towards the school. Once they'd gone through the big oak doors, they headed quickly towards the medieval tower and joined the queue to see the displays.

As they moved through the door into the tower Paige saw a notice explaining that everything on view had been found in the medieval part of the school. Paige saw that the objects were displayed in glass cases, and the girls took a quick look inside each one as they searched for the dress Lily had mentioned.

One case was full of ornate silver buttons, another displayed a beautiful gold and silver casket and some old leather drinking flasks. There was also some beautiful medieval jewellery, set with flashing precious stones.

"There's the dress," Paige said suddenly, pointing at a tall glass case in the corner of the room.

The girls rushed over to look at the dress which was displayed on a tailor's dummy. There was no one else looking at that part of the display, so they were able to get right up close to the glass case.

The dress was made of plum-coloured silk and it had a long flowing skirt, a square neckline and wide sleeves. The bottom of the skirt was trimmed with plum-coloured velvet ribbon running all around the hem.

"Lily was right," Shannon said, looking

tremendously excited. "It's *exactly* the same colour as Velvet's collar!"

Paige and Summer nodded eagerly. The dress looked in remarkably good condition for something which had survived for hundreds of years, Paige thought as they walked around the case, looking at the dress from all angles. There were no rips or stains and the deep, glowing plum colour of the fabric hadn't faded at all.

Suddenly her heart skipped a beat. "Look!" Paige was so excited, she could barely get the word out as she pointed at the back of the dress. "A section of ribbon from the hem is missing," she said. "Could it be—"

"Velvet's collar!" Shannon gasped.

Summer hurried round to the front of the case to read the display notice. "The label says this dress was found when Charm Hall was being turned into a school," she said. "And it's *definitely* from the twelfth century!"

Shannon and Paige scooted round to join her.

"The dress is remarkably well preserved apart from a small section of ribbon missing from the hem," Shannon read aloud over Summer's shoulder.

"This was already missing when the dress was first discovered. It is extremely unusual to find a garment from this period in such good condition, and historians are baffled as to why this particular piece of clothing has survived so well."

Eyes wide, the three girls stared at each other.

"There's something magical going on here," Shannon said softly.

"I wonder whose dress it was," Paige said thoughtfully. "If it was found in the house, maybe it belonged to one of the Charm women."

"Yes," Summer agreed, walking over to read another sign on the wall. "According to this notice, this part of the house is the earliest surviving section, and it was built by a medieval knight who was given the land by the king. The house has belonged to the Charm family since medieval times."

Shannon smiled. "Maybe the girl who owned the dress was Velvet's first owner," she suggested.

"But that would make Velvet over eight hundred years old!" Paige murmured.

Shannon nodded. "Perhaps Velvet's first owner was a witch, like Estelle Charm," she suggested. The girls had learned about Estelle when they'd researched a history project. She had lived in Charm Hall in the seventeenth century, and Lavinia Charm, the founder of the school, had been descended from Estelle's younger brother, James.

Paige's head was spinning as she thought it over, but there was one thing she felt certain of: Velvet's collar *was* the missing velvet ribbon from the hem of the medieval dress.

"Oh, this is so exciting!" Shannon said, her eyes shining, "But it's *killing* me that we don't know anything for sure!"

"Maybe we do," Summer said quietly.

Puzzled, Paige turned to glance at her friend. Summer had moved away to stand in front of a medieval tapestry hanging on the stone wall. The tapestry was old and worn and slightly frayed in places, but the picture was still clear. The tiny glittering stitches showed a beautiful garden scene, filled with bright flowers. A young girl with long fair hair sat by the river, playing a lyre, while behind her a tiny black kitten wearing a plum-coloured collar was chasing a butterfly.

Paige froze as a thrill of recognition shot through her.

"That's Velvet," Summer said, pointing to the kitten in the tapestry. "I'm sure it's her! And do you know what that means?" she demanded excitedly. "It means that Velvet really *is* hundreds of years old!"

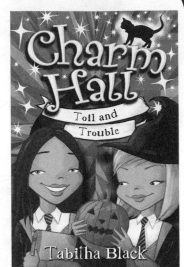

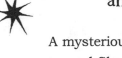

With magic in the air at Charm Hall, this is one boarding school where anything can happen!

A mysterious diary reveals to Paige, Summer
and Shannon that a precious sapphire
is hidden in the school grounds.

Then they discover someone is trying
to steal the jewel! Can the girls –
with Velvet's help - stop them in time

Hodder
Children's
Books

A division of Hachette Children's Books